BUG OFF!

A Swarm
of Insect Words

Cathi Hepworth

G. P. PUTNAM'S SONS · NEW YORK

For Bill and Mike,
who are as cute as a bug's ear!

Copyright © 1998 by Catherine Hepworth
All rights reserved. This book, or parts thereof,
may not be reproduced in any form without permission
in writing from the publisher. G. P. Putnam's Sons,
a division of The Putnam & Grosset Group,
200 Madison Avenue, New York, NY 10016.
G. P. Putnam's Sons, Reg. U. S. Pat, & Tm. Off.
Published simultaneously in Canada.
Printed in Hong Kong by South China Printing Co. (1988) Ltd.
Text set in Times Roman.
Library of Congress Cataloging-in-Publication Data
Hepworth, Catherine.
Bug off!: a swarm of insect words / by Cathi Hepworth. p. cm.
Summary: Presents vocabulary words relating to insects,
including bees, moths, and ants.
1. Vocabulary—Juvenile literature. [1. Vocabulary. 2. Insects.]
I. Title. PE1449.H443 1998 96-31210 CIP AC 428.1—dc20
ISBN 0-399-22640-0
1 3 5 7 9 10 8 6 4 2
First Impression

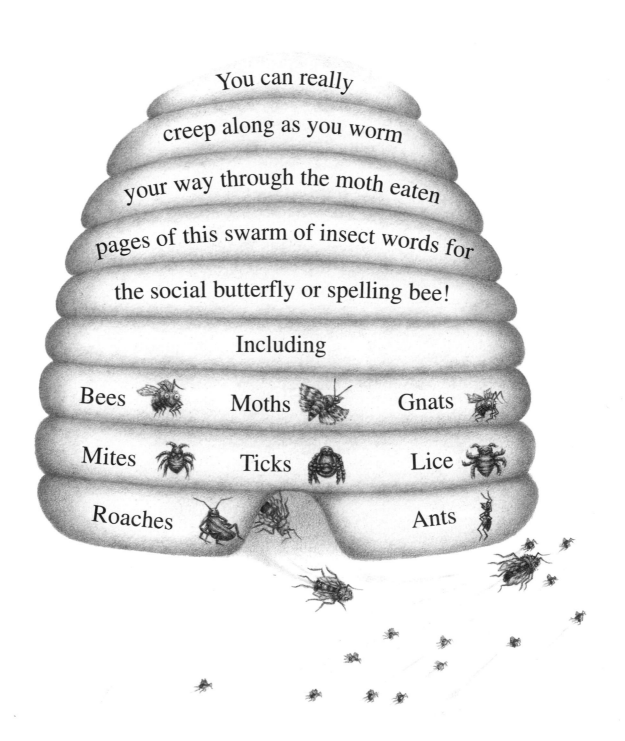

You can really

creep along as you worm

your way through the moth eaten

pages of this swarm of insect words for

the social butterfly or spelling bee!

Including

Bees   Moths   Gnats

Mites   Ticks   Lice

Roaches   Ants

A Real
Fly-by-Night
Operation...

Starring

Bees, Moths, and Gnats

Beeper

Fris**bee**

Beethoven

Bee**fy**

Mam**moth**

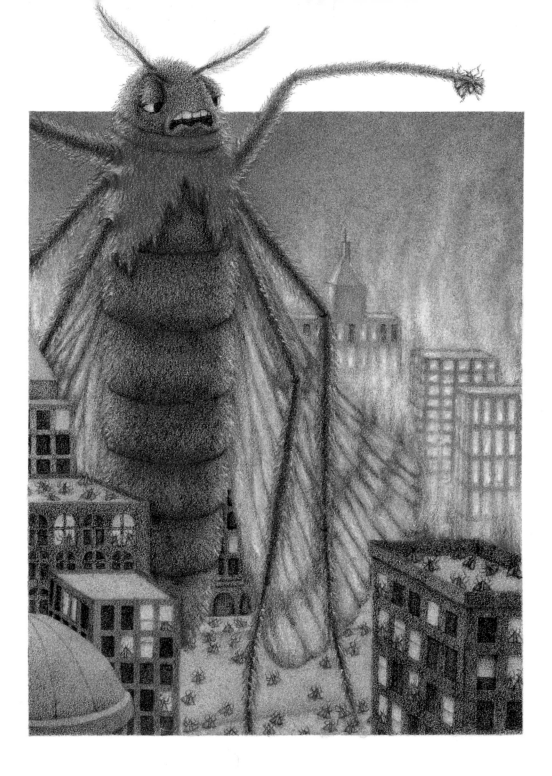

Behe**moth**

Smoth**e**red

Signatures

Stagnate

Don't Let the Bedbugs Bite...

Starring

Mites, Ticks, and Lice

Stalag**mite**s

Dyna**mite**

Ticklish

Broomstick

Tick-tack-toe

DMV CALIFORNIA DMV

DRIVER LICENSE

B7055153   CLASS:C

EXPIRES 2000

BOB, STU, SARA, JANE, JIM, EVE,
AND LEONARD LOUSE
1456 PARASITE PLACE
SAN FRANCISCO CA 94131

EXOSKELETON: YES WINGS: NONE
LENGTH: 1/16" BODY: FLATTENED
LEGS: 6 DATE OF HATCHING: 5-97

SIGNATURES
X X X X X X

05/07/97

1071

License

Slice

The Unwelcome Houseguests...

Starring

Roaches and Ants

App**roach**

Rep**roach**

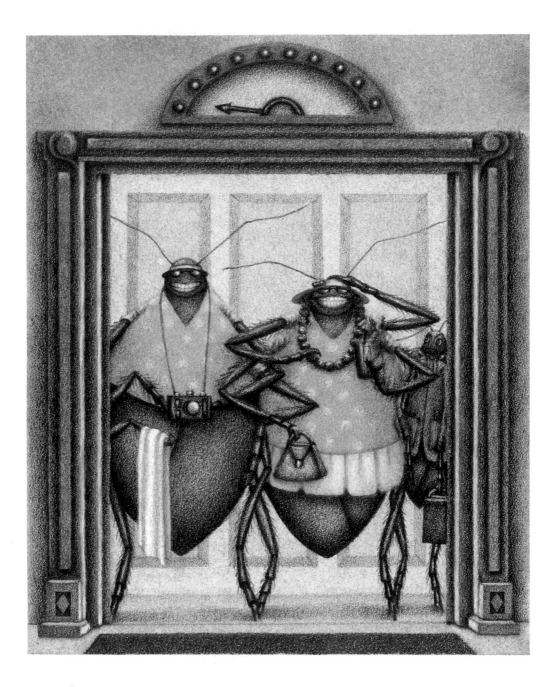

Encroach

Frantic

Rom**ant**ic

Descend**ant**s

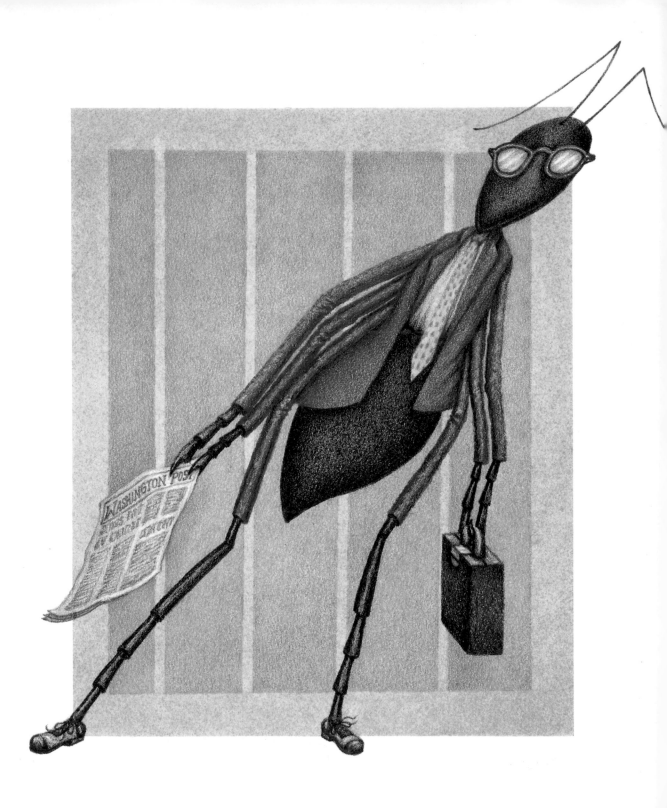

Slanted

Ph**ant**om of the Opera